ACE
THE VERY IMPORTANT PIG

DICK KING-SMITH
illustrations by Lynette Hemmant

CROWN PUBLISHERS, INC.
NEW YORK

J
KIN

Published in 1990 in the United States of America by Crown Publishers,
Inc., a Random House company, 225 Park Avenue South, New York,
New York 10003
Originally published in Great Britain in 1990 in different form by Victor
Gollancz Ltd. as *Ace.*
CROWN is a trademark of Crown Publishers, Inc.
Manufactured in the United States of America

Library of Congress Cataloging-in-Publication Data
King-Smith, Dick. Ace, the very important pig / Dick King-Smith ;
illustrations by Lynette Hemmant. p.   cm. Summary: Farmer Tubbs'
amazing pig, Ace of Clubs, eventually winds up on television for his
cleverness. ISBN 0-517-57832-8 (trade)—ISBN 0-517-57833-6 (lib. bdg.)
[1. Pigs—Fiction.] I. Hemmant, Lynette, ill. II. Title.
PZ7.K5893Ac 1990   [Fic]—dc20   90-1447
                                                        CIP
                                              AC   Rev.

10 9 8 7 6 5 4 3 2 1

First American Edition

91-00645

Contents

ACE
THE VERY IMPORTANT PIG

A Pig with a Mark

"WELL, I NEVER! Did you ever?" said Farmer Tubbs.

He was leaning on the wall of his pigsty, looking down at a sow and her litter of piglets. The sow was asleep, lying on her side, and six of her seven piglets slept also, their heads pillowed on their mother's huge belly.

But the seventh piglet was wide awake and stood directly below the farmer, ears cocked, staring up at him with bright eyes that had in them a look of great intelligence.

"I never seed one like you afore," said Farmer Tubbs. "Matter of fact, I don't suppose there's ever been one like you, eh?"

In reply the piglet gave a single grunt. Farmer

A Pig with a Mark

Tubbs was not a fanciful man, but he did, just for a moment, imagine that the grunt sounded more like a "no" than an "oink." He half expected the piglet to shake its head.

Up till that time the farmer had not noticed anything out of the ordinary about this litter. But what was now catching his attention was the seventh piglet's strange marking, clearly to be seen once he was standing apart from his brothers and sisters. On his left flank there was an odd-shaped black spot.

The sow was a mongrel, numbering among her ancestors Yorkshires and Saddlebacks and Gloucester Old Spots. Usually her piglets were white with bluish patches, but occasionally a baby would be born with an odd spot or two on it, so it was not remarkable that this piglet should have one.

What was extremely unusual was the formation of the single black marking. It stood out clearly against a white background, and it was almost exactly the shape of a club in a deck of playing cards.

"Will you look at that!" said Farmer Tubbs.

"It's a club, a single one! And a card with a single marking is called an ace, young feller-me-lad, d'you know that?"

In answer the piglet gave two quick grunts. Somehow they sounded different from the "no" grunt—sharp, impatient, almost like, "Yes, yes."

"Fancy!" said Farmer Tubbs. "I wonder you never nodded at me." He scratched with the point of his stick at the black marking on the piglet's side.

"There be no doubt," he said, "what us shall have to call you. I don't never give names to piglets as a rule—they don't live long enough to make no odds—but us shall have to name you."

The piglet stood silent and motionless, apparently taking in every word that was said.

"Your name," said Farmer Tubbs, "is written on you. The Ace of Clubs, that's who you be."

For some while longer the farmer stood leaning against the pigsty wall, chatting to the piglet. Farmer Tubbs enjoyed a nice chat, and since he lived alone and saw few other people, he spent a good deal of time talking either to himself or to his animals.

A Pig with a Mark

"If things had turned out different," he said now to the newly named Ace of Clubs, "and I'd married when I were a young man, I'd likely have had six or seven children by now like your mum has. But I can't say as I'm sorry. Maybe it'd have been nice to have a wife to chat with, but you can have too much of a good thing. Only girl I ever fancied marrying, she were a good strong wench and she were a wonderful cook, but my, didn't she go on! Talk the hind leg off a donkey, she could. You couldn't never have a proper conversation with she—you wouldn't get a word in edgeways. We was engaged for a bit, but then she broke it off and went and wed a sheep farmer, long thin fellow name of Hogget. And I'll tell you a funny thing, young Ace of Clubs . . . Are you listening?"

The piglet grunted twice.

"As well as sheep, Hogget had a pig, a huge old white boar, and that boar could round up sheep just like a dog. You wouldn't never think that were possible, would you?"

The piglet grunted once.

"Well, 'tis true," said Farmer Tubbs. "And

what's more, now I comes to think of it, that clever old boar was your great-grandfather! So you never knows, young Ace—you might be an extraordinary pig when you'm full grown."

Except you will never be full grown, thought the farmer. I shall sell you and your brothers and sisters when you'm eight weeks old, and a few months after that you'll all be pork.

He was careful only to think all this and not to say it out loud. Why? he asked himself. Well, the piglet might understand what he was saying, this one might.

Farmer Tubbs's fat red face creased into a great smile, and he shook his head and tapped his forehead with one finger.

"You'm daft, Ted Tubbs, you are!" he cried. "Who ever heard of a pig that could understand the queen's English! Can you imagine such a thing, Ace, eh, can you?"

The piglet grunted twice.

A Pig with a Gift

"MOTHER?" SAID THE Ace of Clubs one morning six or seven weeks later.

"Yes, dear?"

"What's that noise outside the sty?"

"It's the farmer's pickup truck, dear."

"What's he going to pick up, Mother?"

"You, dear. You and your brothers and sisters. To take you for a nice ride."

"Where to, Mother?"

Though the sow knew the correct answer to this question, she did not actually understand what it meant. Over the years, all her children had disappeared to this destination at a certain age, and to be frank, she was always quite glad to see them

7

go. Raising a litter of ever-hungry piglets was *so* demanding.

"You're going to market," she said comfortably.

"What's that?"

"It's a place," said the sow. "A very popular place for a holiday, I should imagine, judging by the number of animals of all sorts that go to market. You'll like it there. You'll make lots of new friends, I expect, and have a lovely time."

Ace's six brothers and sisters grew very excited at these words and ran around the sty squealing. But Ace stood still and looked thoughtful.

"But Mother," he said. "Why do we have to go to market? I like it here. I don't want to go. Why must I?"

"Why must you ask so many questions?" said the sow sharply, and she went into the inner part of the sty and flopped down in the straw with a sigh of relief at the thought of a bit of peace. She listened drowsily to the sounds of Farmer Tubbs rounding up the squealing piglets and putting them into the net-covered back of the pickup truck, and then the noise of it driving away. She closed her eyes and slept.

But when she woke later and went outside again, a shock awaited her. Ace had not gone to market.

"Hello, Mother," he said.

"Why have you not gone to market?" asked the sow peevishly.

"I didn't want to. I told you."

"Didn't want to! It's not a question of what you want or don't want. It's what the farmer wants. Why didn't he take you?"

"I told him. He said to me, 'Do you want to go to market?' and I said no."

"You stupid boy!" said the sow. "How could he have possibly known whether you were saying yes or no?"

Because I've been training him, thought Ace. Two grunts for yes, one grunt for no. I think he's learned that now.

"And how could you possibly have understood what the man said?" his mother went on. "Pigs can't understand people's talk."

"Can't they?" said Ace. That's odd, he thought. I can.

"No, they certainly cannot," said the sow. "No pig ever has and no pig ever will. I never heard such rubbish. But I still can't think why he took the rest and left you."

Just then they heard the sound of the truck returning. The engine was turned off, and footsteps approached the sty.

"There!" said the sow with a sigh of relief. "He's come back for you. He must have overlooked you when he was rounding up the others. You didn't want to go to market indeed! You stupid boy!"

Farmer Tubbs's face appeared over the pigsty wall.

"Don't look so worried, old girl," he said to the huffing, puffing, grumbly sow. "You'll get your rest, all right—I'm taking young Ace away now. Say good-bye to your mother, Ace."

"Good-bye, Mother," said Ace.

"Good-bye," said the sow. Then, feeling she had been a trifle rough on him, she added "dear," and "Have a nice time," and waddled inside to lie down again.

Farmer Tubbs waited a moment, his elbows on the wall top, and looked down at the piglet he had decided *not* to take to market.

"Saved your bacon, I have, for the time being, anyway," he said. "Not that you could know what I'm talking about. Though I daresay you'll get to know what you're called in a while, like a dog would. Eh? Ace! Ace! That's your name, my lad. The Ace of Clubs. Human beings like playing games, you see, and you can play a lot of different games with a deck of cards. Fifty-two of 'em there are in a pack—spades and hearts and diamonds and clubs. Though what good 'tis to tell you all that I ain't got no idea."

He opened the door of the sty and came inside, closing it behind him. The last thing he wanted was the piglet loose in the farmyard, dashing around all over the place. He expected that catching it—even in the sty—might be a job, and that when caught, it would squeal and kick and wriggle as its littermates all had.

"Steady now," he said as he approached the piglet. "We don't want no fuss."

But Ace stood quite still, allowed himself to be picked up, and made no sound or struggle.

"You'm an extraordinary pig, you are, young Ace," said Farmer Tubbs as he carried the piglet out.

Because it lay so quietly in his arms, and because it was already quite a weight to carry, the farmer decided to risk putting the piglet down on the ground outside, so that he could bolt the sty door more easily.

"You sit there a minute, Ace. There's a good boy," he said without really thinking what he was saying, and when he turned around again, it was to find the piglet sitting and waiting.

"Well, I never! Did you ever?" said Farmer Tubbs. "Anybody would think . . . Oh, no, don't be so daft, Ted Tubbs."

He stared at the Ace of Clubs for a long thoughtful moment, and the Ace of Clubs stared back, sitting silently on his heels.

Then Farmer Tubbs cleared his throat, nervously it seemed, took a deep breath, and turning away, said, "Walk to heel, then, Ace." And he set off across the yard. Looking down as if in a dream, he saw the piglet marching steadily along on his left side, its pink snout level with his heels, the strange-shaped black emblem upon its flank showing proudly for all to see.

And perhaps because Ace was marching so smartly, Farmer Tubbs was reminded of his own days as a soldier many years before, and he squared his shoulders and threw out his chest and pulled in his stomach. Left, right, left, right, across the yard he went until they came to the door of a box stall on the far side, and Farmer Tubbs automatically cried "Halt!"

Ace stopped dead.

Inside the box stall the farmer sat hurriedly down on a bale of straw. Strange thoughts rushed through his head, and his legs felt wobbly. He licked his lips and, once again taking a deep breath, said in a hoarse voice, "Ace. Lie down."

Ace lay down.

Farmer Tubbs swallowed. He took a large red and white polka-dotted handkerchief from his pocket and mopped his brow.

"Ace," he said, "listen to me carefully now. I don't want to make no mistake about this. I don't know if I be imagining things or not. I might be going around the bend. It might be just a coincidence, or it might be . . . a miracle. But I got to know for certain sure. So you answer me honestly, young Ace of Clubs. You tell old Ted Tubbs the truth."

He paused, and then very slowly and clearly and loudly (as you would talk to a small child) he said, "Can . . . you . . . understand . . . everything . . . that . . . I . . . say?"

The piglet grunted twice.

A Pig and a Goat

I HOPE YOU can understand something that I'm going to say, thought Ace.

Pigs are permanently hungry anyway, and Ace had not had a mouthful to eat since early that morning, long before the farmer had set out to market. Now he was ravenous, and he let out a short but piercing squeal.

Farmer Tubbs had not kept pigs all his working life without learning that a squeal like Ace's meant either fury or fear or hunger. And since the piglet looked neither angry nor afraid, the farmer got the message and hurried out to fetch food.

"He's not as stupid as he looks," said Ace out loud.

"He'd have a job to be," said a voice.

Ace spun around to see, standing in the gloom at the far side of the box stall, a strange figure. It was covered with long grayish hair that hung down its sides like a curtain, and it wore a gray beard and a pair of sharp-looking curved horns.

The goat walked forward into the light and stood looking down at the piglet.

"What's your name?" the goat asked.

"Ace. Ace of Clubs."

"Funny sort of name," said the goat. "How did you get it?"

Ace turned to show his left side. "It's because of this mark on me," he said. "It's something to do with some game that humans play called cards."

"How do you know that?" asked the goat.

"He told me. Ted Tubbs told me."

"Ted Tubbs? Is that his name? How do you know it is?"

Ace felt like saying "Why must you ask so many questions?" as his mother had, but the goat, with that sixth sense animals have, continued, "I hope you'll forgive me for asking so many questions, but I'm curious to know how you could possibly understand what the man says."

The look in her golden eyes was kindly and mild.

"I just do," said Ace. "I don't know how. I thought all animals did, but my mother said that no pig ever had."

"Nor goat either," said the goat. "Nor cow nor sheep nor horse nor hen, to the best of my knowledge. I've lived here all my life, all fifteen years of it, and the only word he says that I can recognize is my name."

"What's that?"

"Nanny."

Just then Farmer Tubbs opened the door and came in carrying a bucket of pig swill. He poured it into a trough in the corner of the stall and watched approvingly as Ace dug in.

"I'll tell you, Nanny," he said, patting the old goat's hairy back. "You'm looking at a most extraordinary pig there. Not just his markings, I don't mean—I'll swear blind that pig do understand what I say to him."

He waited till Ace had licked the trough clean and turned to face him. Then he said, "Now then, young Ace, allow me to introduce you. This is Nanny, and I'm putting you in with her so's she can keep an eye on you and teach you a thing or two. She's brought up ever so many kids, Nanny has, and there ain't much she don't know. She'll be company for you, stop you feeling lonely."

"What was he going on about?" asked Nanny when the farmer had gone. "I heard my name a couple of times, but the rest was just the usual gabble."

"He said you were very wise," said Ace.

"I wasn't born yesterday."

"And he said he was leaving me in here with you. I hope you don't mind."

"Not a bit," said Nanny. "You'll be company for me, stop me feeling lonely." She pulled a wisp of hay out of the crib and munched it thought-fully.

"How come you never went to market this morning, then?" she said. "I looked out and saw a bunch of pigs going off in the truck. Why did he leave you behind?"

"He asked me if I wanted to go," said Ace, "and I said no."

"You mean to tell me that as well as you being able to understand the man . . . what did you call him?"

"Ted Tubbs."

"As well as you understanding Ted Tubbs, he can understand what *you* say?"

"Only three things," said Ace. "One grunt means no, two grunts mean yes, and a sharpish squeal means 'Fetch food.' I think he's learned those, all right."

"Going to teach him any more?"

"I don't know, really. I suppose I could increase the grunts, three for this and four for that and so on, but I don't know if he could cope with it. What do you think, Nanny?"

"Might be beyond him," said Nanny. "He's not all that bright. Might be better to *show* him what you want."

"Like what?"

"Well, what d'you fancy doing?"

Ace thought.

"I wouldn't mind having a walk around the

farm," he said. "You know, have a good look at everything and meet all the other animals. I've been stuck in a sty all my life so far, and now I'm shut up in here."

"All right," said Nanny. "So you'd like to get out of this stall. I can't open the door, you can't open the door, but he can. I can't tell him to open it, you can. By showing him what you want."

"How?"

"Listen," said Nanny, and she outlined a simple plan.

When Farmer Tubbs next opened the half-door of the box stall and came in to fill Nanny's crib with hay for the night, the old goat bleated. To him it was just a bleat. To Ace she was saying "Go on. Try it now."

Ace trotted up behind the farmer as he reached up to the crib and butted him in the back of the leg with his snout.

"What's up with you, Ace?" said Farmer Tubbs, and for an answer the piglet went to the door that the farmer had closed behind him and butted it hard several times, so that it shook on its hinges.

"You wants me to open it?"

Two grunts.

"Why?"

Ace marched around the stall twice, came back to the door, and butted it again.

"You wants to go for a walk!" said Farmer Tubbs. "Well, I never! Did you ever? What next? D'you want me to come with you?"

One grunt.

"Oh, all right, then. But you come back when I calls you, understand?" And reassured by an affirmative answer, the farmer opened the door.

"And he will," he said to Nanny. "You don't understand what I'm saying because you're not all that bright. But that Ace—why, he can do everything but talk. I suppose you could say he's too clever for words."

A Pig and a Cat

FARMER TUBBS SPENT a worried time talking anxiously to himself as he went about his chores.

"You'm a fool, Ted Tubbs," he said. "Pigs is for pigsties, not to be let go wandering about wherever they fancies. Don't like to follow him around. Looks like I don't trust him. Who ever heard of trusting a pig? I needs my brains seen to. But then he might hurt himself, he might run away, he might get lost. Worth a bit of money a pig that size is, but 'tisn't the value I'm thinking of, to be honest. I've got real fond of that pig."

He kept looking at his watch, forcing himself to allow a full hour to pass, and when it had he went and stood outside the box stall, half hoping

that the pig would have made his own way back
and be waiting there, safe and sound.

But there was no sign of Ace.

Behind Farmer Tubbs there was a rattle as
Nanny put her forefeet on top of the half-door
and peered out.

"Right, then, Nanny," said Farmer Tubbs.
"He's had long enough. It'll be dark afore long.
We'll fetch him back, shall us?" And he called,
"Ace!"

He waited a minute or two, but the piglet did
not appear.

"Coop-coop-coop-coop-coop—come on,
then!" Farmer Tubbs shouted, the sounds he always made to call cows or sheep or chickens. But
though there was some distant mooing and bleating in answer and a few old hens came scuttling
hopefully across the yard, Ace still did not come.

"You'm a fool, Ted Tubbs," said the farmer.
"What am I thinking of? There's only one proper
way to get him back." And he cupped his hands
to his mouth and took a deep breath and bellowed
the summons that all pigmen have always used

over the ages to bring their errant charges hurrying home, curling their tails behind them.

"*Pig*-pig-pig-pig-*pig*! Pig-pig-pig-pig-*pig*!"
roared Farmer Tubbs, and in half a moment there
was a distant rattle of little trotters and Ace came
into sight, galloping as hard as he could go with
that curious rocking-horse action that pigs have.

"What did I tell you!" said Farmer Tubbs
triumphantly to Nanny, but inwardly he heaved
a sigh of relief as he opened the door and let in the
puffing, panting Ace of Clubs.

"Good boy!" he said, patting the piglet. Just
like he were a dog, he thought. "Good boy, Ace!"

But in reply there was only a rather breathless
but nonetheless urgent squeal, so off Farmer
Tubbs hastened to fetch food.

When the farmer—and the food—had finally
disappeared, Nanny said, "How was your walk?"

"I had a lovely time," said Ace. "I made a
speech to the sheep, had a conversation with the
cows, a discussion with the ducks, a gossip with
the geese, and a chat with the chickens. And by
the way, you were right, Nanny. I asked all the

animals if they could understand what Ted Tubbs
says to them, and they couldn't. They know some
things, like to come when he calls them, but that's
about all."

"The cows would know their names, I'm
sure," said Nanny.

"Oh, yes, they did. Named after flowers
mostly, they are—Buttercup, Daisy, Primrose,
that sort of thing. But I'll tell you a funny thing,
Nanny—all the sheep had the same name."

"Really?"

"Yes. I said to one of them, 'What's your
name?' and she said 'Barbara.' But when I asked
the next one, 'And what's your name?' the answer
was 'Barbara.' I asked all of them in turn and they
all said 'Baaaabaara.' "

"How funny," said Nanny, straight-faced.

"Isn't it?" said Ace. He yawned hugely and
snuggled down in the straw.

"Good night, then, Ace," said the old goat.
"Sleep tight, mind the fleas don't bite." But the
only reply was a snore.

Full-stomached and tired after all his exploring

(for his legs were rather short), Ace slept soundly that night. When he woke, it was bright morning and the low early sun was streaming in over the half-door. Ace stood up and shook himself. Nanny lay under the wooden crib, her jaws going around rhythmically.

"Morning, Nanny," said Ace.

"She can't answer," said a voice.

Looking up, Ace saw that there was a cat sitting on top of the crib. It was a large white cat with one yellow eye and one green one.

"Why not?" he said.

"Because she's cudding," said the cat. "Chewing the cud. You're not supposed to talk with your mouth full, didn't your mother tell you?"

"No," said Ace. "Why not?" he added.

"It's rude," said the cat.

At that moment Nanny swallowed noisily and got to her feet.

"Don't tease the lad, Clarence," she said. "He's only young." And to Ace she said, "This is an old friend of mine. His name is Clarence."

"How do you do?" said Ace.

"Pretty well, considering," said the cat.

"Considering what?"

The cat looked narrowly at Ace.

"M.Y.O.B.," he said.

"What does that mean?"

"Mind your own business."

"Clarence!" said Nanny.

"Don't mind him," she went on to the piglet. "It's just his manner. He doesn't mean any harm."

"It's N.S.O.M.N.," said Ace.

"What does that mean?" asked Clarence.

"No skin off my nose."

"You think you're pretty smart, don't you? What do they call you?"

"Ace of Clubs."

The white cat jumped easily down from the crib and walked slowly around the piglet. First he inspected Ace's right (white) side with his left (yellow) eye, and then Ace's left (marked) side with his right (green) eye.

"I've seen that odd black shape somewhere before," he said.

"It's something to do with a game the farmer plays," said Ace. "With some cards."

"Ah, yes, that's it," said Clarence. "He sits down and lays all these bits of card out in rows. I've watched him. He lays them out on the table, some with black marks, some with red, some with pictures."

"Fifty-two of them, there are," said Ace. "Spades and hearts and diamonds and clubs. Funny though, isn't it? I thought you played games with others—I used to with my brothers and sisters, chasing games, tag, that sort of thing. Strange for him to play on his own. He must have a lot of patience."

"Wait a minute, young know-it-all," said Clarence. "Are you telling me you've been inside the farmhouse?"

"Oh, no."

"Then how come you know all this stuff about fifty-two cards and hearts and clubs and all that?"

"He told me. Ted Tubbs told me."

"Ted Tubbs?"

"That's the man's name, Clarence," said Nanny. "You and I have never known what he's called, but Ace found out. You see, he understands the man's language."

"Do you mean to tell me," said Clarence, "that you can understand every word that What's-his-name—"

"Ted—"

" . . . Ted says to you?"

"Yes," said Ace. "I thought that all the animals could, but it seems I'm a freak."

"You'll have to watch out, Clarence," said Nanny. "Next thing you know, you won't be the only one sitting in a comfy chair in the nice warm farmhouse watching Ted play cards. Ace will be in there too."

Clarence gave a loud meow of amusement.

"Not for long," he said. "Young know-it-all wouldn't take much time to blot his copybook."

"What d'you mean?" said Ace.

"Only cats and dogs are allowed indoors, because only they can be housebroken."

"What does that mean?"

With a look of disdain on his face Clarence indicated a large lump of pig dung in the straw.

"You can't go doing that on the carpet," he said. "Or the other."

"Why not?"

"It's rude. Didn't your mother tell you? Humans don't mind if you do it outside, but indoors it's simply not done. We cats bury that sort of thing anyway."

"Oh," said Ace. "Does Ted do it outside, then?"

"No, no, no," said Clarence. "He has a special little room with a kind of white chair with a hole in it."

"He's almost as clean as a cat," said Nanny dryly.

"That would be difficult," said Clarence smugly, and he leaped neatly onto the top of the half-door and was gone.

Ace thought about all this.

"Nanny," he asked, "are you housebroken?"

Nanny gave a loud bleat of laughter.

"Not likely," she said. "A goat's gotta do what a goat's gotta do!"

"Well, d'you think I could be? I wouldn't mind seeing what it's like inside Ted's house. D'you think I could train myself?"

"Ace," said Nanny, "the more I see of you, the more I think you could do most things. Except fly."

A Pig with a Plan

THAT DAY AND every day that followed, Farmer Tubbs let Ace out to run free.

At first Farmer Tubbs bombarded the piglet with a whole list of don'ts—don't go too far, don't go near the road, don't fall into the duck pond, don't chase the hens, and so on. But gradually as time passed and Ace always behaved himself, the farmer just let him out without a word, confident now that he would not get into trouble and would return to the box stall when called. It never occurred to him to say, "Don't go into the house."

In fact, Ace was not in a hurry to do that. He talked the matter over with Nanny, and she advised against haste.

"You don't want to rush him," she said. "Having a pig in the house is not something that humans are used to. He might take it amiss. And one thing's sure—you've got to keep on the right side of Ted Tubbs."

"What's wrong with being on his left side?" said Ace.

"No, it's just an expression. To keep on the right side of someone means to keep in his good grace."

"Good grace? I don't understand."

"Sorry," said Nanny. "You're such a bright fellow that I forget how young and inexperienced you are. What I mean is that it's important for Ted to like you, to treat you as a pet."

"What's a pet?" said Ace.

"An animal that people keep for the pleasure of its company, like a dog or a cat."

"Are you a pet?"

"Sort of."

"What about the other animals on the farm—the cattle, the sheep, and the poultry?"

"No, they're not pets. They all end up as

meat," said Nanny. "Sooner or later young and old alike, they're all killed to provide meat for humans to eat."

Ace shuddered.

"My brothers and sisters," he said, "that went to market . . . ?"

"Someone will have bought them there to feed them till they're fat enough to kill. And that could still happen to you, Ace, if you rub Ted Tubbs the wrong way."

"You mean," said Ace slowly, "if I—what was it Clarence said?—if I blot my copybook?"

"Exactly," said Nanny. "I'm not saying you won't be able to go into the farmhouse one day, if that's what you want to do. But don't try to run before you can walk, don't rush your fences, look before you leap. The first thing to remember is that the farmer is not the only person who lives in that house."

"Why, who else is there?"

"Clarence—and Megan. Now Clarence won't be any problem—I'll have a word with him—but Megan's a different matter."

"Who's Megan?"

"Ted's dog. You may not have seen her. She's not too keen on getting exercise."

"I think I have," said Ace. "Brownish?"

"Yes."

"Short-legged?"

"Yes."

"With big sticking-up ears and a stumpy tail?"

"Yes."

"And very fat?"

"That's Megan. She loves her food, Megan does. She must be the fattest corgi that ever came out of Wales. Now you'll have to get her on your side. You see, cats don't really bother about people, they only care about themselves, but a dog reckons to be man's best friend. Megan could be very jealous. But if she takes a liking to you, I think you'll be home free."

"How can I make her like me?" said Ace.

"I'll tell you," said Nanny. "Megan, you see, is the most tremendous snob."

"What's a snob?"

"Someone who pretends to be much better bred than other folk."

"And is she?"

"No, but she looks down her nose at all other dogs. They are common curs. She says she has royal blood."

"And has she?"

"Ask her," said the old goat. "I'm not going to tell you any more about Megan, because the best thing you can do is to ask her yourself, very respectfully, mind, and remember to appear tremendously impressed by what she tells you. Oh, and don't call her Megan. That would be much too familiar."

"What should I call her?" asked Ace.

"Ma'am," said Nanny.

With all this in mind, Ace began to make changes in his routine. It had become his habit to make, each day, a grand tour of the farm, chatting with all the other animals, for he was a friendly fellow. Meeting the ducks and geese and chickens was easy, for they all ranged freely. As for the cows, the barbed-wire fences that kept them in were no problem for Ace, who ran easily under the lowest strand. Sheep-fencing was a different matter, for by now Ace had grown too big to be called a piglet and was too fat to squeeze through the wire mesh. But this was no great loss, since none of the sheep ever said anything to him but "Barbara."

At first Ace had visited his mother every day to say good morning, but lately he had given this up. For one thing, they could not see each other since the sty walls were too high, and for another, she never really sounded pleased about his visits.

"I understood that you had gone to market," she said when she first heard his voice again. She sounded disappointed. And before long the only answer he received to his cheery greeting was a grunt, so then he didn't bother.

Now he went straight toward the farmhouse as soon as he was let out in the morning, with the idea of meeting Megan in mind.

Behind the house was a lawn bordered by shrubbery, and here he hid to watch what went on. It never varied, he found. Each day when Ted Tubbs had finished milking and gone indoors for his breakfast, the corgi would come out of the house onto the lawn and waddle around on the grass, making herself comfortable. If the weather was fine, she would then lie awhile in the sunshine, but any hint of rain or wind sent her hur-rying in again as fast as her short legs would carry her stout body.

For a week or more Ace lay and watched and wondered how best to approach Megan. First impressions, he felt, might be very important. In any event, the matter was decided for him.

He was lying flat in the shrubbery one sunny morning, watching Megan through the leaves, when suddenly a voice said, "Peeping Tom, eh?"

Ace whipped around to see Clarence sitting a few feet away regarding him with a cold green-and-yellow stare.

"I don't know what you mean," Ace said in a flustered voice.

"Hiding in the bushes," said Clarence. "Spying on a lady. You can't do that."

"Why not?"

"It's rude. Didn't your mother tell you? Just exactly what are you up to, young know-it-all?"

Ace decided on honesty, not because he was aware that it was the best policy but because he was straightforward by nature.

"Clarence," he said. "Will you do me a favor? Will you introduce me to Megan?"

"Why should I?"

"Well, you see, I really am very keen to become a house pig, you know, and live in the farmhouse like you and Megan do. Nanny said that you wouldn't mind but that Megan might not like the idea."

Clarence combed his whiskers thoughtfully.

"You're an odd sort of a chap, you are," he said. "I don't care what you do. As far as I'm concerned it's . . . what was it you said?"

"N.S.O.M.N."

"Quite. And you haven't a hope of succeeding, in my opinion. Never mind what the man thinks of such an idea, I can tell you who won't stand for it, and that's HRH."

"HRH?"

"Her Royal Highness over there—Western Princess of Llanllowell."

"Is that Megan's real name?"

"Oh, yes. Registered at the Kennel Club, ten champions in her pedigree, all that nonsense. It's

43

enough to make a cat laugh," said Clarence, and he stood up and walked out onto the lawn toward the dog, Ace following.

"Megan," Clarence said when he reached her, "this is Ace. Ace, Megan." And he sauntered off, waving his tail.

Ace stood smartly at attention in front of the corgi, his trotters neatly together. Close up, he could see that she was not merely brownish but a fine red-gold color with a snow-white chest.

Ears pricked, head raised, she favored him with an imperious stare. From her expression you would have thought there was a bad smell under her nose.

Ace cleared his throat, and with downcast eyes he said, "Your servant, ma'am."

A Pig and a Dog

♣

THE CORGI DID not reply.

Glancing up, Ace thought that the look in her
eyes had softened a little. Was that a slight wag of
her stumpy tail? Might as well go the whole hog,
he thought.

"Please accept my apologies, ma'am," he said,
"for interrupting your walk. May it please Your
Majesty."

Now the stump was really wagging.

"There's a nice-mannered pig!" said Megan.
"Sick and tired it is we are of being called plain
Megan by that cat. Who was it told you that we
are of the blood royal?"

"A friend, ma'am. Nanny the goat."

"The goat!" said Megan scornfully. "A creature of no breeding whatsoever. Common as muck. Surprised it is we are that she should even be aware of our rank. What did she tell you about us?"

Ace had never heard of the royal "we," but he was becoming used to the way the dog spoke and to her unfamiliar lilting accent, so different from Ted Tubbs's broad tones.

"She said you had a very good pedigree, ma'am," he said. "Though I don't quite know what that means, I'm afraid."

"We don't imagine for one moment that you would," said Megan.

She stared pointedly at the mark on Ace's left side.

"You're not pure bred, that's obvious, isn't it?" she said.

"I shouldn't think so," said Ace.

"Don't know anything about your ancestors, we presume?"

"No. Though I'm told my great-grandfather was a sheep pig."

"Well, there you are, see. Doesn't bear thinking about."

"But please," said Ace, "won't you tell me all about your family, ma'am? If you would be so gracious, Your Majesty."

"There's ignorant you are," said Megan. "There's only one person in the whole country who is properly addressed as Your Majesty, and that is the queen. She is the most important human being in the land, see. Now, the point about our family is not merely to do with pedigree—plenty of dogs have pedigrees a mile long, even if not as distinguished. No, the reason why we are head and shoulders above all the other breeds is this: Corgis are the queen's dogs. Buckingham Palace is bursting with them, and wherever the queen goes—Windsor, Sandringham, Balmoral—she takes them with her.

"Now, the queen's children are called Their Royal Highnesses. In fact, she made her eldest son the Prince of Wales—because of her fondness for corgis, no doubt. And so her own dogs are styled princes and princesses every one. Now, it so happens, see, that we personally are directly related to the royal corgis. Western Princess of Llanllowell, that is our proper title."

"So should I call you Your Royal Highness?" said Ace.

"No, no, that's for humans. Corgis were originally bred as cattle dogs, to nip at their heels. Now, a tall dog might get a good kick in the face doing that, but our breed, see, has nice short legs to keep out of trouble. So it's plain how you should address me, isn't it, now?"

"How?"

" 'Your Royal Lowness,' " said Megan. "But you need only do so at the start of a conversation. From then on, 'ma'am' will suffice."

"Yes, ma'am," said Ace.

"Now," said Megan, "the audience is at an end. You may attend on us tomorrow."

"Yes, ma'am," said Ace.

He turned to go, but Megan said sharply, "Backwards, look you."

"Sorry?"

"It is customary to withdraw backwards when leaving the presence of royalty."

Ace could not wait to tell Nanny. He raced back to the box stall and bashed so loudly on the door with his hard little snout that a puzzled Ted Tubbs came hurrying to let him in.

The farmer leaned on the half-door and looked at the pig.

"What's the matter, my boy?" he asked. "Did something frighten you?" But receiving only a single grunt in reply, he went off again about his business.

"What was he saying?" asked Nanny.

"He was asking if something frightened me. But I was just in a hurry to come in because I've just met Megan and I'm bursting to tell you all about it," said Ace, and he did.

"Your Royal Lowness indeed!" said Nanny. "What a fraud! She really gets my goat with all her airs and graces. Are you going to be able to put up with all that stuff, Ace?"

"Oh, yes, it's quite amusing, really. I didn't realize a snob would be so funny."

"I suppose she said that you were common?"

"Oh, yes, and you too."

Nanny gave a snort.

"D'you think," said Ace, "that Megan is really related to the queen's corgis?"

"Shouldn't think so for a moment. What she has never realized is that it doesn't matter *who* you are. It's *what* you are that counts in this life, and you're worth ten of that silly fat thing. Snobbery apart, she's like all dogs—thinks she can understand what the man says. But like all dogs, she can't. Just a few commands that she's learned to obey. That's about as far as it goes. Now you, you can understand his every word. Did you tell Megan that?"

"No."

There was a scratch of claws on the outside of the half-door, and Clarence appeared over the top of it.

"She wouldn't believe you if you did," he said.

"Oh, you heard that, did you?" said Nanny.

"Listening in on other people's conversations!" said Ace. "You shouldn't do that, Clarence."

"Why not?"

"It's rude. Didn't your mother tell you?"

Clarence did not answer this. Like all cats, he had the knack of making others feel uncomfortable by simply not reacting, by appearing, that is, to be taking no notice of what has been said. He jumped up onto the crib and began to wash his face, so that now it was Ace who felt that he had been rude. He tried to make amends by making conversation.

"Why wouldn't Megan believe me, Clarence?" he asked.

Clarence finished his washing before replying.

Then he said, "Because she only believes what she wants to believe. Besides, if you succeed in your plan to get into the house, you could have the upper hand. You'll be able to understand the man. She won't. It could be amusing."

"Now, Clarence," said Nanny. "I know what you're thinking. You'd like to take that dog down a peg or two, wouldn't you?"

Once again Clarence did not answer. He lay down and licked his black nose with his pink tongue. Then he wrapped his white tail around him, shut his yellow eye, shut his green eye, and went to sleep.

The next morning, when Farmer Tubbs came out of the house after breakfast, he saw a strange sight. Sitting close together in the middle of the lawn

were his dog, his cat, and the Ace of Clubs. Anyone would think, he said to himself, that all three
of them were household pets.

"You'll have to watch out, Megan, and you,
Clarence," he said. "Next thing you know, you
won't be the only ones sitting in comfy chairs in
the nice warm farmhouse, watching me play
cards. Ace will be in there, too." And he walked
away chuckling to himself at such a ridiculous
idea.

A Pig in the House

♣

THE FARMER'S WORDS, Ace could see, were received quite differently by the other two animals. Clarence took absolutely no notice but stared absently into the distance. Megan looked up at the man, her ears flattened, and wagged her whole rump in pleasure at the sound of his voice.

Pity she can't understand what he said, thought Ace. She might ask me in. Ted's left the door wide open, too. How am I going to wangle an invitation? He caught Clarence's eye (the yellow one, as it happened), and once again that telepathic sense that humans seldom have but animals so often possess came into play.

"He's left the door open," said Clarence. "Care to have a look around the house, Ace?"

"Oh, could I?" said Ace. Clarence had never

before called him by name, and he warmed to the white cat.

"You most certainly could not!" barked Megan sharply. "A pig in the house! That's ridiculous! We never heard of such a thing!"

"I just thought you might like to show Ace your trophies, Megan," said Clarence smoothly.

The corgi's expression softened.

"Trophies?" said Ace. "What are they?"

"Awards that Megan won at dog shows," said Clarence. "Prize cards, rosettes, that sort of thing."

"And a cup," said Megan. "You're forgetting that we won a cup in our younger days."

"So you did," said Clarence. "A little silver cup. Well, silvery-colored, anyway. Ace would be ever so interested, wouldn't you, Ace?"

"Oh, yes, yes, I would! You must be very proud, ma'am, to have won those things."

"We hardly expected to lose," said Megan, and she got up and waddled off into the farmhouse.

"Come on," said Clarence. "That's tickled her vanity. I knew it would. Follow me, now, and don't speak till you're spoken to."

Inside he led the way down a passage and into the living room. On either side of the fireplace was an armchair, and in the smaller one the Western Princess of Llanllowell already lay in regal state.

On the wall beside this chair were pinned three cards, colored red, with black writing on them, and tacked to each card was a blue rosette. On the mantel above the fireplace stood, among other knickknacks, a very small cup of a size suitable to contain a sparrow's egg.

Megan glanced up at these objects.

"The royal collection," she said offhandedly. "Beautiful, isn't it, now?"

"Oh, yes, ma'am," said Ace in a reverent tone. "It is an honor to see them."

See them he could, but read what was written on them he could not. The inscription on the three prize cards was in fact identical except for the dates, which spanned three successive years:

VILLAGE FAIR

NOVELTY DOG SHOW

CLASS 10   FATTEST DOG

FIRST PRIZE

A Pig in the House

On the little cup was engraved:

DOG DERBY
ANY VARIETY 200-YARD RACE
BOOBY PRIZE

"Impressive, aren't they?" said Clarence. He winked his green eye at Ace.

"Oh, yes!" breathed Ace.

"Gracious of Her Lowness to compete, don't you think?" said Clarence, shutting his yellow eye.

"Royalty has its obligations, look you," said Megan modestly. "Noblesse oblige."

She settled herself more comfortably in the armchair.

"The cat will take you on a conducted tour," she said. "We hope your feet are clean."

"Oh, it was a scream, Nanny!" said Ace that evening back in the box stall.

"Clarence just went out of the room, of course, but I could see Megan watching me out of the corner of her eye, so I walked out backward.

" 'What does "noblesse oblige" mean, Clarence?' I said when I caught up to him.

" 'It's foreign talk,' he said.

" 'What sort?' I said.

" 'Double Dutch,' he said.

"So I wasn't any the wiser."

"Never mind," said Nanny. "What happened next?"

"Clarence showed me all over the house."

"Upstairs too?"

"Yes, though that was difficult. The stairs are steep. Megan can't get up them at all, Clarence says—she's too stout. I saw the bedrooms, and a room with a big white trough in it. That's where Ted washes himself, and there was one of those white chairs with a hole in the middle of it, too. There was another one in a very small room downstairs as well."

"You didn't . . . do anything, I hope?" said Nanny.

"Do anything?"

"Yes, you know . . ."

"Oh, no," said Ace. "I went out on the lawn. 'I'll be in the kitchen when you're finished,' Clarence said to me. He's nice when you get to know him, Clarence is, isn't he?"

"Yes," said Nanny. "He lives in the kitchen, I know. He has a bed right by the oven. He's often told me how cozy it is there on winter nights."

"That's right," said Ace. "I saw some other downstairs rooms, but the kitchen's lovely, full of nice food smells. Still I think the living room's the place for me, even though it means putting up with Her Lowness."

"Why?"

"Because in the living room Ted Tubbs has got the most amazing thing, Nanny. You just can't imagine what an extraordinary thing it is."

"What is?"

"The magic box!"

"Magic box?" said Nanny. "What are you talking about, Ace?"

"Well," said Ace, "when we'd finished the tour of the house, we went back into the living room and Megan asked Clarence if he'd showed me everything, and Clarence said yes and Megan said 'Upstairs too?' And then Clarence stared at her in that way he has and said 'Oh, yes, Your Lowness, the stairs weren't too high for Ace,' and Megan said 'We are not amused,' and Clarence said 'A cat may look at a princess' and climbed into the other armchair.

"I waited a bit but neither of them said any more. In fact they both went to sleep, so I thought maybe I'd outstayed my welcome. But just as I was going out of the room I saw this thing in the corner. A big box it was, only one side was nearly all glass, like a window. So I walked up to it and looked in this window, but all I could see was myself looking back."

"That would be your reflection," said Nanny. "Like you get if you look in a puddle or in the duck pond. Nothing magic about that."

"No, but wait," said Ace. "Below this glass window there were some knobs sticking out. So out of curiosity I pushed one of those knobs with my snout, and you wouldn't believe what I saw then, Nanny!"

"What did you see?"

"Inside that box," said Ace slowly and impressively, "there was a man talking! He was talking about all kinds of different things, and as well as the man there were loads of different pictures, and the man talked about them, too. Megan and Clarence didn't take a bit of notice, I suppose because they wouldn't have understood what the man was saying. But I could, of course, and it was ever so interesting, Nanny, honestly! I tell you I simply couldn't take my eyes off that magic box!"

Thus it was that Farmer Tubbs, his morning's work finished, came into his living room to find the Ace of Clubs sitting on his heels in front of the television set watching the one o'clock news.

A Pig and the Television

♣

AFTER THAT, LIFE was never really the same again
for Farmer Ted Tubbs. All that afternoon he
talked to himself in a bemused fashion.

"That pig," he said, "he were sat there watching the telly! Must have switched it on hisself.
Never seed such a extraordinary thing. I couldn't
think of nothing to say. In the end I says to him
'Anything interesting on the news, then, Ace?'
and he gives a couple of grunts, so I didn't like to
turn it off. I goes and has my bit of lunch and
when I comes back he's sat there watching *Neigh-
bours*. What next, Ted Tubbs, what next?"

So stunned was the farmer by the pig's actions
that the idea of forbidding him to enter the house
in the future never crossed his mind, especially

because in the days that followed Ace behaved faultlessly. All he did was to watch a great deal of television. He damaged nothing and made no messes anywhere (for Farmer Tubbs had the sense always to leave the door to the garden open: he himself often did not bother to take off his boots when he came in, so a few muddy pig-trotter marks did not signify). And in the afternoon, before the farmer came in after finishing the afternoon milking, the pig would turn off the television with a prod of his snout, leave the house, and make his way back to the door of the box stall. Here, if Farmer Tubbs did not hurry, a loud squeal would tell him that Ace wanted to be let in, fed, and left to spend the night with his friend Nanny the goat.

"Just as well, I suppose," the farmer said to himself (and to Megan and Clarence, though his reasoning meant nothing to them), "because if he stayed in the house we'd have the telly on all night long. 'Tisn't that I don't enjoy some programs, but when there's rubbish on, I likes to switch off and have a nice game of solitaire. Now if that pig was in nights, he'd be watching the midnight movie and then he'd have the telly on till 'twas time for milking again."

In point of fact, Ace was becoming very selective in his viewing. He had not been a house pig many days before he found out, first by chance and then by trial and error, that pressing each of the five knobs below the window of the magic box produced a different result. One turned the thing off, and the other four controlled four different channels. Ace of course had no idea that there were such things as different channels, but he soon found that the magic box offered a choice of pictures. His sense of time was good, too, and after a few weeks, his viewing had taken on a definite pattern.

By experimenting with the control knobs, Ace found what programs suited him and at what time of day. These generally were split into two parts: morning viewing and afternoon viewing. In between, he took a nice long nap, lying on the hearth rug. He had the sense not to attempt to get onto either of the armchairs.

For his morning watching—that is, between the hours of roughly 9 A.M. and 11 A.M.—he usually chose a program for schools called *Daytime on Two,* where there was a section called "Look and Read" and items on such things as science and mathematics. All of these Ace found fascinating, though on occasion he would switch to Channel Four's *Our World,* which often had interesting information about food.

In the afternoon, say between 4 P.M. and 5:30 P.M., Ace enjoyed children's TV. There were always plenty of animals, both live and in cartoons, and their antics amused him.

But though the afternoon's viewing was for fun, the morning's, because of his unique gift for understanding the human tongue, was, for Ace, highly educational, especially with regard to numbers and to language.

Quick to learn, Ace began to recognize simple words. There were, for instance, items about road safety, using diagrams with large lettering, and soon Ace, had he been called upon, could have distinguished a sign that said STOP from one that said GO.

Soon, too, he acquired a basic grasp of figures,

becoming aware, for example, that he had one snout, one tail, two eyes, two ears, and four legs, and that the sum of himself and the other two animals was three.

At first Ace feared that Clarence and Megan might object to his generous use of the television set. By good fortune, however, he found that though in general they were not interested, certain items appeared that were popular with them.

Clarence enjoyed the cat food commercials, particularly one that showed a large white cat very much like himself fishing meat from a can with one paw in the most elegant manner.

As for Megan, luck had it that quite early on, BBC 1 showed a repeat of a program about the day-to-day life of the royal family. There were pictures of the queen and her husband and children and grandchildren at Buckingham Palace, at Windsor, at Sandringham, and at Balmoral, and everywhere she was surrounded by corgis.

The moment Ace heard the program announced, he woke Megan.

"Quickly, Your Lowness, quickly!" he cried.

"The queen is in the magic box!" And sure enough, there she was, in the opening shot, walking in her garden with no less than six corgis.

Megan's growl at being disturbed changed to an eager whine.

"Oh, there's lovely, see!" she said excitedly. "Our aunt Olwen that is, by the queen's feet, we're nearly sure! And the one behind her looks ever so like our cousin Myfanwy!"

She watched spellbound as the program continued, silent except for an occasional yap at recognizing an uncle or a grandparent, and when it was all over she actually, for the first time, addressed the pig by his name.

"Our thanks to you, Ace," she said graciously. "We shall be obliged if in the future you will draw our attention to any more pictures."

"Of the royal family, you mean, ma'am?" said Ace.

"Of *our* royal family, yes. If the queen appears without them, don't bother to wake us."

None of Ace's viewing bothered Ted Tubbs, for he was always busy around the farm. Like all farmers he could not treat Sunday as a day of rest. The cows still needed milking morning and evening, babies were born regardless of the day of the week, and all the animals needed bedding and food and water.

But Farmer Tubbs did treat Sunday differently in one way. He always tried to finish his morning's work by eleven o'clock, and then he set about preparing and cooking himself a large traditional Sunday lunch.

It never varied. Roast beef and Yorkshire pudding, roast potatoes and green vegetables and lashings of thick gravy, followed by a jelly roll. While this was cooking, the farmer would pour himself a quart mug of cider and, sitting in the larger of the two armchairs with his feet up, would drink it slowly with much lip smacking and a belch or two for good measure.

But on the very first Sunday after he had discovered Ace watching the television, the scene in his living room was different.

Anyone looking in through the window would not have been surprised to observe the farmer in one chair and his dog in the other, but might well have been amazed to see, sitting at the farmer's side, a sizable young pig, a white pig that bore on its left side a curious mark shaped like the ace of clubs. Farmer Tubbs took a gulp of his cider and addressed his house pig.

"Now then, Ace," he said. "I been telling my-self these last few days that maybe old Ted Tubbs is going daffy. You was sat in front of the telly when I come in t'other day, there's no doubt of that. And the telly was switched on, there's no doubt of that. But I must have left it running. I can't believe 'twas you as switched it on."

He took another drink, bracing himself for what he had to do.

"I got to find out for sure," he said. "I don't never have the thing on this time of a Sunday, so I don't know what rubbish they be showing, but lunch won't be ready for another half hour, so we might as well turn it on. Or rather you might as well turn it on, Ace. I hopes you can, for my peace of mind."

He raised his mug, took a long swallow, and then, pointing at the television set, said in as firm a voice as he could manage, "Switch it on, Ace. Any channel will do."

Later on, when Ace's morning lessons had taught him to read what was written beneath the control knobs—the numbers 1, 2, 3, 4, and finally the word OFF—he might have selected a channel.

71

As it was, with luck once again on his side, he simply walked over to the set and pushed the middle one, three.

"The time," said the announcer as he swam into sight, "is exactly twelve thirty. Time for our regular Sunday program especially for those of you who earn their living from the land. Sit back, put your feet up, and for the next half hour enjoy *West Country Farming,* followed by *The Farmers' Weather Forecast.*"

Ted Tubbs's mouth fell open. He stared in wonderment at Ace.

"Well, I never!" he said. "Did you ever?"

A Pig in a Pickup

♣

ON A SUNDAY evening some months later, Ace lay in the straw of the box stall telling Nanny, as he always did, about the day's viewing.

No longer did he refer to the magic box. He had learned that what he was watching was a television set, which could show pictures of things that were happening all over the world and even from space. How the television did this remained to him, as it does to most humans, a mystery, but he did not worry his head about that. It was full enough already of ideas and impressions and new-found knowledge.

Much of what he told the old goat meant little or nothing to her. Her experience of life was, after all, very limited, for she had never moved a step outside Ted Tubbs's farm. But she listened with interest to his stories of strange lands and peoples and customs and a host of other things shown on the educational programs.

Since it was Sunday, Ace and Ted had of course watched *West Country Farming* while the lunch was cooking, and now the pig could not wait to tell Nanny all about the program. It had upset him deeply.

Indeed he left half his supper untouched, and his voice trembled as he told her what he had seen.

"Oh, it was horrible, Nanny!" he said. "The first part wasn't too bad. It was about a market. I used to think that my brothers and sisters had gone to a town called Market, but these were pictures of pigs, sheep, and cattle in pens, and people offering money for them. 'Bidding,' it's called—the one who offers the most money gets the animals. I must say I'm glad I didn't go to market, but at least all the beasts there were still alive and well. But the second half of the program—ugh!"

It wouldn't be true to say that a shudder ran through Ace's body. His flesh was too solid for that, but if he could have shuddered, he would have.

"Why?" said Nanny. "What was it about?"

"An abattoir!" said Ace in a funereal voice. "A slaughterhouse, where animals are taken to be killed. They didn't show that part, thank goodness, but they showed all the bodies. Rows and rows of them there were, all hanging head down, strung up by their back legs, cattle, sheep, and pigs."

"Goats?" said Nanny.

"Don't think so. The cattle and the sheep weren't too dreadful because by then they were just sides of beef or carcasses of lamb, but the pigs still looked like pigs. Dozens of them were hanging there, all scrubbed and cold and still. I won't sleep a wink tonight."

"Humans have always killed animals," said Nanny.

"Not only animals," said Ace gloomily. "You should just watch the television. Humans spend a lot of time killing other humans."

"Not for food, surely?" said Nanny.

"No, I don't think so, but the news is nearly

always about people getting killed. Sometimes they do it on purpose, with guns and bombs, and sometimes they get killed by mistake on trains or airplanes or on the roads. And as well as that, there are natural disasters like earthquakes and floods, and thousands of people die."

"Sounds very depressing, watching television," said Nanny.

"Oh, it isn't all like that," said Ace. "Sometimes it's quite funny. There's a program that Clarence especially likes called *Tom and Jerry*."

"Who are they?"

"Tom's a cat and Jerry's a mouse."

"Another program about sudden death?"

"No, because, you see, Tom is stupid and Jerry's very smart, so Jerry always gets the best of things. Clarence likes the parts where Tom gets his tail caught in a door or gets beaten up by a bulldog, that sort of thing."

"Don't you ever feel," said Nanny, "that you'd like to stay in and watch the evening programs? Or stay the night, perhaps? I mean, don't think I'm trying to get rid of you—I love having you here—but there must be a lot of television you've never seen yet."

"No, thank you," said Ace. "I did stay a bit later than usual one evening—it was after *Tom and Jerry* and Clarence was telling me how he would deal with Jerry and what a dumb cat Tom was—and I found that it's about then that Megan wakes up. She sleeps most of the day, but when it's getting near her suppertime she comes to life, and oh, Nanny, she's such a *bore*! On and on about all the champions in her pedigree and how her niece was presented at Court and what the Queen Mother is supposed to have said to her uncle Gareth. No wonder Clarence goes out every evening. No, daytime viewing is enough for me, and anyway, I like talking it over with you afterward. But I hope I don't have nightmares tonight. Ugh! That slaughterhouse!"

"Look, Ace," said Nanny. "I am a great deal older than you. Which doesn't make me wiser, because you've already learned a whole host of things about the world that I had no idea of. But I do know one thing, which is this: Worrying does no one any good. Hundreds of thousands of pigs may get slaughtered, but you won't. With a bit of luck you and I are both going to die quietly and peacefully in our beds of old age. I shall die before you, just because I am a great deal older, but I don't worry about it. So finish your supper."

"I think I will," said Ace, and he did.

"Now then," said Nanny, "you come and lie down."

She settled herself near him, but not too close, for he had grown quite heavy.

"I won't sleep," said Ace.

"Try counting sheep," said Nanny. "Live ones. That'll send you off."

"I don't think it will," said Ace, but it did.

Though Ace did not exactly have any nightmares, he did have a strange dream. He dreamed that he was riding in Farmer Tubbs's pickup truck. The farmer was driving with Ace next to him on the passenger's side, held there by some kind of arrangement of straps. Where they were going he did not know, but in the dream he was able to get his tongue around some of the words of the English language that he had come to recognize on the "Look and Read" program.

"Where are we going, Ted?" he asked, and the farmer replied, "To market."

Two days later, a Tuesday, it was market day, and Ace stood in the yard, watching idly as Farmer Tubbs came out of a shed carrying a calf, which he put under the net in the back of the pickup. Then he looked at Ace. Then he said, "I be going to market, Ace. Want to come?"

Remembering his dream on Sunday night, Ace replied with a single explosive grunt, a very definite "No!"

But by now, after many months of communication with the pig, Farmer Tubbs was completely confident that Ace understood every single word he said, in a way that no dog, let alone Megan, ever could, not even the most intelligent dog in the world. Now he came up to Ace and fondled the roots of his big ears, something that he knew the pig greatly enjoyed.

"Now you listen here, my boy," he said. "There ain't no need for you to come if you don't want to. I just said to myself, 'Ted Tubbs,' I said, 'maybe Ace would enjoy the ride. And 'twould be company.' Now, I reckon I know what's worrying you. You think I might be going to sell you, isn't that it?"

Two grunts.

"Never, Ace, never," said Farmer Tubbs earnestly. "You got my solemn oath on it. I won't never part with you and that's a promise. You believe that, don't you?"

Two grunts.

"That's all right, then. Now then, time I was off," said the farmer, and he opened the passenger door.

"You coming?" he said, and to his delight Ace, with a final couple of grunts, jumped into the truck and sat upright while Farmer Tubbs carefully fastened the seat belt around Ace's fat stomach.

A Pig in a Pub

THE FIRST PAIR of eyes to see Ace as he rode along in the pickup truck were very shortsighted ones. They belonged to an elderly lady who was the village gossip. She lived with her sister in a cottage next to the road that led from the farm to the market town. All day she sat and peered out between her lace curtains, minding everyone else's business.

"Quick!" she called as the pickup approached. "Look at this!" But by the time her sister arrived, the truck had passed.

"Oh, you're too late!"

"What was it?"

"Ted Tubbs on his way to market—I recognized his truck. And what d'you think, he had a woman with him! He's kept that quiet, hasn't he? These old bachelors! You can't trust them!"

"What did she look like?"

"Well, I couldn't see her face too well, my sight's not what it was, but I can tell you she was a big stout piece, and no beauty neither."

A small boy playing in his front garden was the next to see Ace. The pig's bulk hid the man from the child's sight, and greatly excited, he ran indoors, crying, "Mommy, Mommy, I've just seen a pig driving a truck!"

"Don't be silly," said his mother.

"I did! I did!" yelled the boy angrily.

"Don't tell lies," said his mother, "and don't you shout at me like that!"

A minor accident was the only other thing that happened on the journey to market. A driver approaching a traffic light suddenly caught sight of Farmer Tubbs's passenger. Goggle-eyed, he turned his head to watch them pass and ran neatly into the back of the car ahead.

When Farmer Tubbs arrived in town and reached the market, he drove the pickup into the parking lot. This was close to the tavern, a pub

called the Bull, used by all the farmers and dealers and truck drivers to quench their thirst on market days.

"Now," said Farmer Tubbs to Ace, "I has to take this here calf in, and then I shall have a look around and see what the trade's like. So will you be all right sitting here for a bit?" And when he received an affirmative answer, he undid Ace's seat belt for greater comfort, shut the door, and went off with the calf.

Ace looked all around him with curiosity, but though he could hear a good deal of mooing and bleating and grunting, he could not see much of interest through the windshield except lots of cars and trucks and Land-Rovers.

Presently, for something to do, he moved along the seat and arranged himself on the driver's side. Often on Saturdays he had watched Formula One car-racing on *Grandstand,* and though the pickup was hardly a Grand Prix car, there were certain likenesses. It had a steering wheel, and a gearshift, and an instrument panel. Raising his front legs, Ace rested his trotters on the steering wheel and gave himself up to a daydream of being the world's first Formula One pig racecar driver.

At that moment a red-faced man came rather unsteadily out of the Bull and began to weave his way across the parking lot.

"Why, if it isn't old Ted Tubbs!" he cried as he neared the pickup, but then the color drained from his cheeks, leaving them as gray as cold porridge, and he staggered away murmuring to himself, "Never again! Not another drop!"

After an hour or so Farmer Tubbs returned. Though he had left the pickup's windows open a little, he found Ace panting, for the metal cab was not the coolest of places on a warm day.

"You'm hot, Ace!" said the farmer. "You'm thirsty, too, I daresay?" And Ace assured him, in the normal way, that this was indeed the case.

"Tell you what," said Farmer Tubbs. "I always has a drink in the Bull afore I goes home on market day. You come in along with me, and we'll ask the pub manager for some water for you. I gotta bucket in the back."

Thus it was that the patrons of the Bull were treated to the sight of Farmer Tubbs entering with a large pig at his heel.

"Now, now, Ted," said the pub's manager. "You can't bring him in here. You seen the notice on the door."

"I did, Bob," said Ted Tubbs. "No dogs allowed, it says. This here's a pig."

"That's true," said the manager thoughtfully. "The usual for you, then? Half of scrumpy?"

"If you please," said the farmer.

Farmer Tubbs was a very moderate drinker. Cider was his usual, but only on Sundays before lunch did he allow himself that quart mug. A half pint was his ration, especially on market days when he was driving.

"What about your friend?" said the manager.

The farmer held out his bucket.

"Put some water in here, will you, Bob?" he said.

"Go on, Ted!" someone shouted. "Buy 'im a beer. You can't bring the poor beast into a pub and not give him a proper drink."

"He shall have one on the house," said the manager, and he drew a pint of beer and poured it into the bucket.

Ace, who had been listening carefully to these exchanges, noted with pleasure that the name on the pump handle was that of a brand highly recommended in the television commercials.

He bent his head to the bucket.

The beer looked good.

He put his snout in the bucket.

The beer smelled good.

He drained the bucket.

The beer tasted good.

He gave a short happy squeal, and it was obvious to everyone what he meant.

There came a chorus of voices.

"He liked that!"

"That were a drop of good stuff, old chap, weren't it?"

"Same again, that's what he's saying!"

"He could do with the other half!"

"And one for the road!"

And the drinkers in the public bar rose, to a man, and poured their tankards of beer into Ace's bucket.

Almost before Farmer Tubbs had tasted his

half pint of cider the pig's bucket was empty again, and when they left, it was with some difficulty that the Ace of Clubs managed to get back into the pickup truck.

"Good thing you're not driving," said the farmer as he strapped the pig in.

Ace hiccupped.

At first the drive home was uneventful, but then fate decreed that a police car should come up behind them just as Farmer Tubbs swerved wildly across the road. He swerved because Ace had fallen asleep and despite the seat belt had lurched sideways against him.

The next moment there came the sound of a siren, and then the police car, lights flashing, pulled in front of the pickup and forced it to a stop.

One of the two police officers in the car got out and walked to the driver's side of the truck. Farmer Tubbs rolled down his window. The smell of beer inside the truck was overwhelming.

"Good afternoon, sir," said the police officer in the coldly polite way that police officers have on these occasions. "Having trouble with the steering, are we?"

" 'Twasn't my fault," said Farmer Tubbs. " 'Twas the pig."

"I see," said the officer. He produced his breath-analyzing kit.

"Now, sir," he said, "I'm going to ask you to blow into this tube. If you look at this machine, you'll see that there are three little lights on it—just like traffic lights—green, amber, and red. Now then, sir, if the green light comes on when you blow, that means you have had no alcoholic drink at all."

"Well, I have had," said Farmer Tubbs. "A half pint of cider in the Bull."

The police officer raised his eyebrows at this. The amount the farmer cited was within the allowable limit. But he wrinkled his nose at the stench of beer drifting out the window.

"In that case," he said, "the amber light will come on. This is to show that you have drunk alcohol in some shape or form. But if, after forty seconds, that amber light should go off and the *red* light come on, then, sir, you will be over the limit and I shall have to ask you to accompany me to the station for a blood test."

Farmer Tubbs shook his head in pity.

"You'm barking up the wrong tree, young man," he said. "I shan't never be over the limit."

"Just blow, sir," said the police officer. "Anyhow, it's never safe to drink any alcohol before you drive," he added as a stern warning. "Then we'll see."

So he did, and they did.

The amber light came on. The police officer watched, waiting for it to change to red, confident that here was yet one more drunken driver. A half pint of cider indeed! But after forty seconds the amber light went out and no red light appeared.

"I don't understand it," said the officer. He went and fetched the second constable from the police car.

"The stink of beer in there's enough to knock you down," he told his partner.

" 'Tis the pig," said Farmer Tubbs.

At this point Ace awoke, roused by the sound of voices. He looked happily at the six men he

could see, four police officers and two Farmer
Tubbses. He gave an enormous belch, and both
police officers reeled backward.

"Well, I never! Did you ever?" said Farmer
Tubbs. "Ace, you've gone and made a proper pig
of yourself!"

A Pig in an Armchair

♣

"TELL YOU ONE thing," said Farmer Tubbs as they drove on home. "With all that beer inside you, I reckons you better go straight in the box stall. We don't want no accidents in the house, do we, Ace?"

Ace let out two sleepy grunts. He had meant to give a single one, but he seemed not to be quite in control of things.

"Oh, no, we don't!" said Farmer Tubbs, and when they reached the farm he drew up outside the box-stall door.

"It don't matter," he said, "if you wets your bed in here."

Nanny was peering out.

"He's had a skinful, Nanny," said the farmer.

Once the seat belt was undone, getting out of the truck was more a matter of falling out for Ace, and he walked into the box stall in a rather wobbly way. Nanny bleated anxiously.

"Don't you worry," said Farmer Tubbs. "He'll be all right when he's had a good sleep."

Ace did indeed fall fast asleep.

While he slept, Clarence came to visit.

"Oh, Clarence, I'm worried!" said Nanny. "There's something the matter with Ace. He wasn't acting at all naturally. What can it be?"

Clarence was a cat of the world. More than once he had courted the Blue Persian at the local pub, and the smell of alcohol was familiar to him. "He's had a skinful, Nanny," Clarence said. And when the simple old goat still looked mystified, Clarence explained.

"Today," he said, "this little piggy went to market, and by the look of things, he drank a good deal of beer. He'll be all right when he's had a good sleep."

Neither the farmer nor the cat was quite correct. Ace did have a good sleep, but when he woke he was not quite all right.

"Oh, Nanny!" he groaned. "I've got an awful headache!" And after a while he explained all that had happened.

"I must have drunk a whole bucketful," he said.

"Why did you drink so much?" asked Nanny.

"I was so thirsty. And it did taste nice. But now I wish I hadn't."

"Well, you've learned a lesson," said Nanny. "A little of what you like does you good. But you can have too much of a good thing."

Clarence was in the kitchen when Ace went into the farmhouse on the following morning. He got out of his bed by the oven and walked around the pig, looking critically at him with first the green eye, then the yellow eye.

"Better?" he said.

"Oh, yes, thanks, Clarence," said Ace.

The white cat sat down in front of Ace and gave him a quizzical green-and-yellow stare.

"Seen Megan yet this morning?" he asked.

"No. Why?"

"She was wondering where you were yesterday."

"Did you tell her?"

"Stupidly, I did."

"Why stupidly?"

"Because I suspect Her Lowness is just longing to take you to task about your behavior," said Clarence.

He gave a fair imitation of Megan.

" 'Going into a pub, look you, and drinking too much, see! There's *common!*' I would stay out here and miss her if I was you."

"Oh, but it's Wednesday," said Ace.

"So?"

"*Paddington Bear* is on. I always watch that."

"I wish you luck," said Clarence.

Ace tiptoed into the living room, hoping to find Megan asleep. She was, so he turned on the TV very softly (he had long ago learned to operate the volume control with his teeth). But before Paddington could appear, the telephone rang, something that always woke the dog, for she considered it her duty to boost its sound with a volley of barks.

This double summons brought Farmer Tubbs in from the yard, and when he had gone out again after answering the call and leaving muddy boot marks across the carpet, Megan lost no time in speaking.

"We want a word with you, boyo," she said sharply.

The old Ace would have replied to this in the meek, respectful way in which he had long been used to speaking to the corgi. "Yes, Your Lowness?" he would have said, and perhaps added, "What is it, ma'am?"

But now a sudden flame of rebellion burned in Ace's broad breast. You stupid pompous little beast, he thought, with all your airs and graces, speaking to me as if I were no better than a . . . a dog. Western Princess of Llanllowell, my trotter! Why, you're just a mouthy little Welsh cow hound. What am I doing kowtowing to you? And he did not answer.

"Did you hear what we said?" snapped Megan.

"Not now, Megan," said Ace firmly. "I'm busy."

There was a short stunned silence before the Western Princess found her voice.

Then, "Upon our word!" she spluttered. "*Not now,* indeed! *Busy,* indeed! *Megan,* indeed! You will kindly address us in the proper fashion."

At that moment Paddington appeared on the screen in his funny blue hat.

"Oh, shut up!" said Ace, and he turned the volume up full.

"Oh, Nanny, you should have seen it!" said Clarence that night. Often he came in the small hours for a chat with Nanny, who like many old folk did not sleep well. Now he had jumped up to his usual perch on the crib, where on occasion he launched himself upon an unwary mouse. Ace was fast asleep in the straw.

"Megan was jumping up and down in her chair," Clarence went on, "yapping her head off, practically frothing at the mouth, and Ace just turned his back on her and sat watching till his program was over. Then he switched it off and turned around.

" 'What was it,' he said very quietly, 'that you wanted to say to me?' Well, by now her ladyship was so hopping mad at being treated so disrespectfully I thought she was going to have a fit.

" 'How dare you tell us to shut up!' she yelled. 'How dare you!' "

"And what did Ace say to that?" said Nanny.

"Oh, it was great!" said Clarence. "He got up and he walked slowly over to where she was sitting, in the smaller of the two armchairs, and he said, still very quietly, 'I'll tell you how I dare. It is because I have suddenly realized that I am no longer a little piglet, bowing and scraping to you, and having to listen to you talking about your piffling pedigree and your rotten relations and what the Princess of Wales said to your great-aunt Fanny. I am now a large pig, about ten times as large as you, and I am fed up to the back teeth, of which I have a great many'—and he opened his

mouth wide—'with all your silly, snobbish nonsense.' "

"And what did Megan say?" asked Nanny.

"He didn't give her a chance to say anything,"
said Clarence. "He did all the talking. 'Now,' he
said, 'I want to watch *Time for a Story* on Channel
Four, and I do not wish to be interrupted. On
second thought, get out of this room. Just push

off, quick!' And he gnashed his teeth together with a very nasty noise that sounded like *Chop-Chop! Chop-Chop!*" I don't think Megan's moved so fast in years. She couldn't exactly put her tail between her legs—there isn't enough of it—but she was out of that room like a . . . like a . . ."

"Scalded cat?" said Nanny.

"Exactly. And," said Clarence, "this is the best part. Ace switched on Channel Four, and then he climbed up into Ted's big armchair and sat there watching. Then after the program was over and all was quiet again, Megan came slinking back. Oh, Nanny, how are the mighty fallen! She stuck her head around the door and gave a little whine, as if to say, 'Please, may I come in?' "

"What did Ace say?" asked the old goat.

The white cat looked down with a certain fondness at the sleeping pig, the strange black mark on his side rising and falling to the rhythm of his breathing. Clarence was not one to give his affection easily, but he had grown to like the Ace of Clubs.

"I thought he handled it beautifully," he said.

"He could have gone on being tough with her—
'I'm bigger than you, watch your step'—that sort
of stuff. Or he could have got a bit of his own
back on her for the way she's always patronized
him—teased her or sneered at her for her high-
and-mighty ways. But no, he just said quite firmly
but in a kindly voice, 'Come in, Megan. I've
something to say to you.'

" 'Yes, Ace,' said Megan rather uneasily. You
could see she was expecting him to tell her off
again, but instead he said, 'There's a documentary
about Cruft's dog show on the telly this afternoon. They've just shown a clip of it, and there
were quite a lot of corgis there. I wondered if
you'd like me to switch it on for you when the
time comes?' "

"What did she say?" asked Nanny.

"She looked at him," said Clarence, "just like
she looks at her master. She put her ears flat, and
she wagged her rump, and she said in a humble
voice, 'Oh, we should like that, Ace! There's kind
of you.'

"Oh, I wish you could have seen him, Nanny,

sitting in that big armchair, looking for all the world like Ted Tubbs's twin brother. He sat there staring down at Megan, and what d'you think he said to round it all off?"

"What?"

" 'There's a good dog, Megan. There's a good dog.' "

A Pig in the Papers

♣

ON MARKET DAY the following week the Bull was, as usual, full of farmers and dealers and truck drivers. In addition there was a very young man who had just started in his first job as a cub reporter for the local newspaper, *The Dummerset Chronicle*.

One of his duties was to cover the market and take note of the livestock prices, not the most interesting work. So he pricked up his ears, as he sat in a corner nursing a glass of lemonade, at a conversation between the pub manager and some of the customers.

"Ted Tubbs been in with that pig, Bob?" asked one.

"Ain't seen him today," said the manager.

"I never seen nothing like that afore," said another.

"A pig drinking beer like that!" said a third.

"I reckon he put down more than eight pints," said the manager.

"He had a skinful," said the first man.

A pig drinking beer, said the reporter to himself. Though he had not been long in the job, he knew that an interesting item of news that you got before anyone else was called a scoop, and he hastily swallowed his drink and hurried off to the newspaper offices.

"It might make a story," said his editor in the tired, bored way that editors have. "Go and see this Farmer Tubbs and find out what you can."

When the cub reporter arrived at the farm and rang the front doorbell, no one answered. This was partly because Farmer Tubbs was busy with the afternoon milking and partly because the bell hadn't worked in years.

So the reporter walked around to the side of

the farmhouse, where he found the garden door open. Someone had the television on, he could hear, so he walked in, calling, "Hello? Excuse me! Can I come in?"

From the nearest room a dog barked, but then came the sound of a single loud grunt and the dog immediately fell silent.

Nervously, for he felt that perhaps he had already gone too far, the young man opened the door to the room.

Though in later years, as a much-traveled reporter, he saw many strange sights in many strange countries, he never forgot the scene that now met his eyes.

On the television was the cartoon *Tom and Jerry*.

Directly in front of the TV set sat a white cat, its tail swishing angrily (for Jerry had just caught the tip of Tom's tail in a mousetrap).

In a small armchair lay a very fat corgi.

In a big armchair sat a large pig.

All three were watching the cartoon.

All three took not the slightest notice of him.

"Oh, I like *Tom and Jerry*! said the cub reporter. "Can I watch, please?"

And almost as though it was some sort of reply, the pig grunted twice.

"Who was that?" said Ace after the young man had left to try to find the farmer.

"Haven't a clue," said Clarence, and "We don't know, we're sure," said Megan.

"He likes *Tom and Jerry* anyway," said Ace.

"How do you know?" said Megan.

"He said so."

"Of course!" said Megan. "We were forgetting." For she now knew of Ace's great gift. The old Megan would never have believed in the possibility of such a thing. The new Ace-worshipping Megan had no doubt at all of his powers.

Across the yard the hum of the milking machine suddenly stopped.

"I'm going for my supper," said Ace. "Shall I switch the telly off?"

"Sure," said Clarence, and "There's kind of you!" said Megan, so he did.

Hardly had the reporter found the farmer and introduced himself than there came the sound of a loud, urgent squeal.

"Just a minute, my lad," said Farmer Tubbs. "Time and tide and Ace wait for no man." And he hurried off to fetch the pig's supper.

The old man and the young leaned on the half-door of the box stall, watching.

"He's enjoying that," said the cub reporter. "Is there any beer in it?"

"Bless you, no!" said Farmer Tubbs. "Why ever . . . ? Oh, I see. You've heard tell, have you? When he had a few in the Bull?"

"Yes. And I'd like to do a story on it for the *Chronicle,* if you don't mind, Mr. Tubbs. A pig that drinks beer, that'll make a nice little item, half a column maybe, and it'd be quite a scoop for me. I've just started the job, you see."

"Who told you about this?" asked the farmer. "The police?"

"The police? No, I heard it in the Bull. What's the pig's name, by the way?"

"The Ace of Clubs."

The reporter looked at the mark on the pig's side.

"Oh, yes, I can see why," he said. "If I write about it, it would be good publicity for you, Mr. Tubbs. You should get a really good price for him then."

"I will never sell him," said Farmer Tubbs. "He's a pet. A house pig, that's what he is."

"That reminds me," said the reporter. "You must have left your TV set running. No one answered the bell, so I went in through a side door and the pig was watching TV along with your dog and cat."

"He enjoys a bit of telly," said the farmer.

"That'll make the story even better. You'll be telling me next that he selects the channels and switches it on himself, ha, ha!"

"Ha, ha!" said Farmer Tubbs.

"By the way," said the reporter, "the pig was sitting in an armchair, your armchair, I daresay."

"Ah, now that explains something," said the farmer. "Lately I said to myself, 'Ted Tubbs, you must be putting on weight something cruel—the springs in this chair have gone flat. You'll have to go on a diet,' I said. Ah, well, that's a relief."

By now Ace had finished his supper. He stood

and looked up at the two men with bright eyes that had in them a look of great intelligence, and when Farmer Tubbs said, "Did you enjoy that, old chap?" he grunted twice.

"Anyone would think he could understand what you were saying!" said the reporter.

If only you knew, thought the farmer, but you ain't going to. You can write a piece about him having a drink or watching the telly, but nobody except me is ever going to know that my Ace do know every word that I do say to him. Folk would never believe it, anyway. They'd take me away from here and put me in the funny farm.

"You write your piece, young man," he said, "and mind and let us have a copy."

And sure enough, the very next day a copy of *The Dummerset Chronicle* was delivered to the farm.

A PIG IN A MILLION

Of all the pigs in England's green and pleasant land, surely none can compare with the Ace of Clubs, belonging to local farmer Ted Tubbs.

Not only does Ace have the freedom of Mr. Tubbs's picturesque old farmhouse, he also enjoys watching television, sitting at his ease in the farmer's armchair.

The Ace of Clubs has been to market, but only as a passenger in Farmer Tubbs's truck. Not only does his unusual pet enjoy the outing, he also savors a refreshing drink of beer at the market's popular hostelry, the Bull Inn. But not for Ace the pint mug. He drinks his beer by the bucket.

"I'll never part with him," Farmer Tubbs told our reporter. "He's a pig in a million."

At lunchtime that day Ted Tubbs read this to Ace, who later translated it for Clarence and Megan and, that evening, for Nanny.

"I shall have to have that framed," said the farmer, "and put on the wall alongside Megan's prize cards. Pity they never done a photograph. I'd like to have a good one of you."

The very next day farmer Tubbs's wish was granted, for a phone call came from one of the national newspapers, wanting to send an interviewer and a photographer, and in due course a large section of the British public opened their copies of the *Daily Reflector* at breakfast time to see a fine picture of Ace, carefully positioned in profile to show his distinguishing mark to best advantage. The picture was accompanied by a generous if somewhat inaccurate piece which stated that Ace drank a gallon of beer with every meal, that he not only sat in an armchair but slept in the spare bed, and that his favorite programs were *University Challenge* and *Mastermind*.

But this was not all.

A week later the BBC called.

"Mr. Ted Tubbs?" said a voice.

"Speaking," said the farmer.

"This is the producer of *That's the Way It Goes*."

"Oh, yes."

"You have heard of the program, of course."

"Can't say I have."

"You haven't heard of *That's the Way It Goes*, presented by Hester Jantzen on Sunday evenings at nine thirty?"

"Oh, bless you, young man, I don't watch telly that time of night. I be abed by nine. I has to get up early to milk the cows. Early to bed, early to rise, makes a man healthy and wise if it don't make him wealthy."

"Well, this won't exactly make you wealthy, Mr. Tubbs," said the producer, "but we can offer you a fee and certainly pay all your expenses for first-class travel and four-star accommodations if you and your pig would be willing to come to London."

"Whatever for?"

"Why, to appear on *That's the Way It Goes.* Hester Jantzen is greatly looking forward to interviewing you both."

"Well, I never!" said Farmer Tubbs. "Did you ever?"

A Pig on the Stage

A LITTLE LATER there came a letter from the BBC, giving the date and time and various arrangements. Farmer Tubbs told Ace all about it, and afterward Ace told his friends.

"What d'you think!" he said excitedly to Clarence and Megan. "Ted and I are going to London!"

"To see the queen, is it?" cried Megan.

"No, no, we're going to be on the telly. Just think, you'll be able to sit here and see us on the box."

"Except that we can't switch the thing on," said Clarence.

"I'll show you how to do it, Clarence," said

Ace. "Look, just put your paw on this knob—where it says 'one'—and push. See?"

"How in the world are you going to get to London, Ace?" asked Megan. "It's a long way, look you."

"Oh, the BBC is arranging everything," said Ace. "They're sending one of the station wagons that their film crews use—Volvos they are, you've seen them in commercials. There'll be loads of room for me in the back—and that will take us straight to the studios. Then when we've done the program, they've booked a room for Ted for the night, in ever such a posh place."

"Buckingham Palace?" said Megan.

"No, no, a big hotel near Regent's Park."

"Where will you sleep?" asked Clarence.

"Well," said Ace, "they seemed to think I might not be happy in the hotel, so I will be sleeping in the London Zoo. Remember, you've seen pictures of it on the telly? And in the zoo they have what they call Pets' Corner. That's where I'm going. And then the next morning we'll be picked up and driven back home again."

"That's all very well," said Megan with a return of some of her old spirit, "but who'll be looking after us?" (And by "us," she meant, of course, herself.)

"One of Ted's friends is coming in," said Ace, "to do the milking on Sunday afternoon and Monday morning and feed all the animals. It'll be a lovely break for Ted."

Because for many months now the dog and cat had had so much explained to them of what appeared on television, they were able to imagine what Ace would be doing. But trying to explain things to Nanny was not so easy.

"They're going to put me on the television," he said to her that evening after supper.

Nanny of course had never in her long life set hoof inside the farmhouse, so that the only idea of the television she had was what Ace had originally told her—that it was a big box with one side nearly all glass, like a window.

"Put you on the television?" she said. "But surely you'll smash the thing? It'll never bear your weight."

Ace tried his best to explain to the old goat all

that was going to happen, but many of the words he used—"Volvo," "London," "studio," "cameras," "hotel," "zoo"—meant nothing to her.

"Oh, well, just as long as you enjoy yourself, Ace dear," she said, "that's all that matters."

And enjoy himself the Ace of Clubs most certainly did when the day came.

What a day it was!

First there was the journey. Ace's trips in Ted Tubbs's rattle-bang old pickup truck had not prepared him for the luxury of travel in a huge modern warm silent comfortable car speeding eastward along the expressway, and because of his modest ability in reading and numbers and his interest in road-safety programs on the television, there were many signs and billboards that caught his eye. One, though, at a roadworks, puzzled him. DEAD S OW, it said, and the missing *L* led him to fear the worst.

Oh, but when they reached London—the streets, the houses, all the thousands of buildings! Their numbers filled him with amazement. In all his six months of life he had only been in two houses, a private one—the farmhouse—and a public one—the Bull Inn—and he stared in wonder at the acres of concrete and tar.

But London, he could see, was not completely built over. There were a number of large grassy spaces with fine trees, and as they passed through one of these parks Farmer Tubbs asked the driver to stop for a moment. It occurred to him that this Hester Jantzen person might not be pleased if Ace had an accident during the interview, so he let Ace out for a little walk.

Then at last they arrived at BBC Studios!

How the onlookers gaped as the pair of them stepped from the staff car to make their entry.

Ted Tubbs was dressed to the nines. Bathed and shaved so closely that his chins bore several little cuts, he had attired himself in his best. Not only was his shirt clean but it had attached to it something he normally never wore—a collar. Moreover, he had put on his one and only tie (a black one, so useful for funerals), and in place of boots he was shod in a pair of old but well-polished black leather dress shoes.

But the crowning glory was his suit. It was

his only suit, of a color best described as sky-blue, which he had bought as a young man. There was no hope of buttoning the jacket, though by letting out the backstraps of the vest he had been able to button that up. As to the trousers, most of the buttons were safely in position, and where the top ones refused to meet he wore, concealed beneath the vest, a carefully attached short piece of binder twine.

And if the man was at his smartest, what of the pig?

Ace positively shone. Not only had Farmer Tubbs hosed him down and soaped and scrubbed him all over, but when the soap was rinsed away and Ace had dried in the sunshine, the farmer had produced a big bottle of vegetable oil and greased the pig all over.

Gleamingly clean, the single mark on his left side showing up more blackly than ever under its sheen, Ace marched proudly into the reception area at his master's heels, and they were conducted to the hospitality room.

Farmer Tubbs was asked what he would like to drink.

"You won't be on camera for a while yet," his hosts said. "So can we offer you some refreshment?"

It being Sunday, Ted had had his quart of cider before lunch, as usual, but he felt thirsty after the journey, and anyway it struck him that a drink might lend him courage, for he was nervous.

"Well, thank you," he said. "I'll have a half pint of scrumpy."

"Pardon?" they said.

"Cider," he said. "Dummerset cider. We come up from Dummerset where the cider apples grow. And the pig'll have a pint of your best bitter."

Farmer Tubbs's cider, when they brought it, was horrid weak sweet stuff, but Ace had no complaints about the beer. They poured it into a bowl for him, and he thoroughly enjoyed it. But he remembered Nanny's words—"A little of what you like does you good. But you can have too much of a good thing." And when they offered him another pint, he gave just one grunt.

"He don't want no more," said Farmer Tubbs. "And neither do I."

A Pig on the Stage

For a while longer they waited in the hospitality room (whence all but they had fled). Farmer Tubbs grew steadily more nervous. The sweet cider had done him no good. Ace, on the other hand, was on top of the world. The pint of beer had made him feel happy and carefree, and he could not wait to go in front of the cameras. The fact that millions of people would be watching did not worry him, because he didn't realize that they would be. He was simply thinking of Clarence and Megan at home, hoping that Clarence would remember to turn on the TV, and only sorry that dear old Nanny wouldn't see him.

So that when they came to the hospitality room to tell Ted Tubbs it was time to go on stage, Ace hurried out ahead of his master. Brushing past the guide who was to take them to the set of *That's the Way It Goes,* he heard a woman's voice saying, "And now, ladies and gentlemen, allow me to introduce . . ."

That's me, Ace thought, and pushing through some curtains, he arrived onstage just as a woman with her back to him completed her introduction.

". . . Farmer Ted Tubbs!"

There was a huge roar of laughter from the studio audience as a large pig appeared.

Hester Jantzen clapped her hand to her mouth in astonished embarrassment, and a second roar of laughter came as Farmer Tubbs, helped on his reluctant way by a push, arrived on the stage looking, apart from his clothes, like the pig's twin brother.

Hester Jantzen took her hand from her mouth and smiled, revealing, Ace could see, a fine set of teeth. She was dressed in a silk dress of a shade of emerald-green that clashed horribly with the farmer's sky-blue suit, and for a moment it seemed as though a clash of a different kind might occur, for Farmer Tubbs did not know why everyone was laughing at him, and whatever the reason, he did not like it. Already nervous and uncomfortable in his too-tight clothes, he now felt the heat of the studio lights, and his red face turned redder still.

Hester Jantzen, professional to her painted fingertips, took command of the situation. Gliding forward, she shook the farmer's large sweaty hand and with another flashing smile said, "Welcome

to *That's the Way It Goes,* Mr. Tubbs. How good of you to come and to bring your famous pig, the Ace of Clubs."

She turned to the camera. "Many of you watching," she said, "will have read in the newspapers about Farmer Tubbs's pet, Ace to his friends. We've had some unusual animals on *That's the Way It Goes* before, but never one as big, I think."

She made a half move as though to give Ace a pat as he stood patiently in the middle of the stage, but the sheen of oil on his bristly back deterred her, not to mention his size.

"He's a whopper, Mr. Tubbs," she said with a light laugh. "How heavy is he?"

"Ten score," grunted the farmer.

"Ten score? What does that mean?"

Farmer Tubbs took out a large, polka-dotted handkerchief and mopped his streaming brow. These London folk, he thought angrily, they don't know nothing.

"Don't you know what a score is, young woman?" he said.

"Why, yes. Twenty."

"Well, now we're getting somewhere," said

Farmer Tubbs. "A score be twenty pound, so ten score be two hundred. Not difficult, is it, really?"

The audience roared.

Now they were laughing at her, not him, and he sensed this. He began to think he might enjoy himself, and Hester Jantzen sensed that.

"Silly me!" she said. "Tell us some more about him. I'm told he likes a drink of beer. Would he like one now?"

"He's had one, out the back," said Farmer Tubbs. "That's enough to be going on with."

Hester Jantzen put on her most roguish smile.

"Just as well," she said. "We don't want this little piggy to go wee-wee-wee all the way home."

"Don't you fret, young woman," said Ted Tubbs. "He'm housebroken, like you and me."

When Hester Jantzen could speak above the studio audience's laughter, she said, "I'm told that the Ace of Clubs does a number of remarkable things, apart from beer drinking, such as sitting in an armchair and watching television."

"He's a extraordinary animal," said the farmer.

"I can see that. People don't realize how

knowing pigs are. I believe it was Sir Winston Churchill who said 'A dog looks up to man, a cat looks down to man, but a pig will look you in the eye and see his equal.' "

"He knowed a thing or two, old Winnie did," said Farmer Tubbs. "You have a good look in Ace's eyes, young woman. You'll see what he meant."

Gamely Hester Jantzen forced herself to approach the Ace of Clubs. They stared at each other, and it was she who looked away first.

"He has a look of great intelligence," she said a little shakily. "Tell us, Mr. Tubbs, what else can Ace do?"

"Whatever I wants him to."

"You mean, like sitting down or lying down or coming when he's called?"

"Them's easy things," said the farmer. "Sit down, Ace," and Ace sat down.

"Take the weight off your feet, my lad." And Ace lay down—on his left side, as it happened.

There was loud applause from the studio audience, and Hester Jantzen clapped her hands.

"Roll over, Ace," said Farmer Tubbs, "and show them how you got your name."

As Ace obeyed, one of the camera operators quickly zoomed in to show a closeup of that extremely unusual single black marking for all the millions of viewers to see.

"Good boy," said Farmer Tubbs. "Now, in a minute or two, I want you to go over to Miss Wassername there and say 'Thank you for having me.' "

"You're not going to tell me," the host said, giggling, "that Ace can speak!"

"No, nor fly neither," said the farmer, "but he'll shake hands with you. Go on, Ace, say thank you to the lady."

And then, before the wondering gaze of the studio audience and all the viewers across the length and breadth of England who were watching *That's the Way It Goes,* the Ace of Clubs walked solemnly across the stage and, sitting down on his haunches, raised one forefoot and politely offered his trotter to Hester Jantzen.

Bravely the lady grasped it.

"Good-bye, Ace," she said. "I do hope you've enjoyed yourself. Have you?"

And the pig grunted twice.

A Very Important Pig

♣

AS SOON AS the BBC staff car dropped them back at the farm on Monday morning Ted Tubbs hurried to change into his greasy old overalls and his dungy old boots to go around and make sure that his animals had not suffered any harm while in the care of a stranger.

Ace made his way to the living room, where he found Megan alone.

"Hello, Megan!" he cried. "We're back! Did you enjoy the program?"

"Indeed to goodness, no!" said Megan.

"Why not?"

"Never saw it, see. Clarence must have pressed the wrong knob. Sat there for ages waiting for you to appear, we did, and all they showed was a lot of cowboys and Indians."

A Very Important Pig

Later, when the cat appeared, he favored the pig with a rather cold green-and-yellow stare, as though daring him to mention the matter, so Ace didn't.

But Fortune decreed that nothing was lost. When Farmer Tubbs came in for his lunch, he turned on the one o'clock news, and farmer, pig, dog, and cat sat and watched as at the end of it the newscaster said, "Finally, for those who say the news is all doom and gloom nowadays, here is a clip from last night's edition of *That's the Way It Goes*." And there was Ace having his trotter shaken by Hester Jantzen.

"A nationally known celebrity," said the newscaster, "greets a brand-new one."

In the days and weeks that followed, it became apparent just what a celebrity Ace had become. Only once, many years before, had a pig appeared on TV and attracted anywhere near as much publicity, and that was when Ace's great-grandfather had defeated all the best dogs in the land to win the Grand Challenge Sheepdog Trials.

Farmer Tubbs was bombarded with letters

and phone calls. Fan letters made up much of the mail, addressed to:

The Ace of Clubs
c/o Mr. T. Tubbs

The mail brought invitations to Ace to open festivals as well, or even new supermarkets, or to appear at functions as a VIP (Very Important Pig). And there were many offers to buy him for large sums of money from farmers everywhere and from more than one circus proprietor. There was also an offer of marriage (for Mr. T. Tubbs) from a lady in Weston-super-mare.

But Farmer Tubbs refused all these things.

The thought of parting with his pig never crossed his mind.

"You got your health and strength, Ted Tubbs," he told himself as he finished the afternoon milking one day, "and you got your livestock to see to, and your pets—old Nanny and Megan and Clarence and, above all, that there Ace of Clubs. What good would any amount of money be to you if you had to part with him? Why, you wouldn't have no one to watch *West*

Country Farming with. You wouldn't have no one to keep you company in the old pickup. You wouldn't have no one to enjoy a drink with at the Bull."

He turned off the milking machine, and almost at once he heard, from the direction of the box stall, a short but piercing squeal, a squeal that he well knew was not of fury or fear but of hunger, and he hurried away obediently to prepare a bucket of pig swill.

As for Ace, success did not spoil him. He had his friends, his favorite television programs both educational and entertaining, his occasional pint, his comfortable bed. After supper that evening he lay thankfully down in it, ready for a good twelve hours of sleep. It was odd, but he always slept on his right side, as though to show to all whom it might concern that mark emblazoned on his left.

" 'Night, Nanny," he said, yawning.

Dimly he heard the old goat reply as she always did: "Sleep tight. Mind the fleas don't bite." And then, with a last couple of grunts, the Ace of Clubs drifted happily into dreamland.